W0007082

# Coloring the Rainbow

## A Story about the Power of Connection

Catherine Rose

Illustrated by Jeffrey Dale

## About the Author

Catherine Rose is enjoying that time of life when one thinks of creating a legacy. As a retired pediatric nurse with advanced degrees in public health and holistic nursing, Catherine understands the effect that a positive self-image has on supporting children to become the best versions of themselves. She draws on life's lessons to write stories with empowering messages to benefit the health and well-being of the generations to follow.

She writes from the back porch of her log home, inspired by the backdrop of Mount Jefferson in Ashe County, North Carolina. Married to her high school sweetheart, she enjoys perpetual recess with their two grandchildren.

Learn more about Catherine and her books at www.catherinerose-childauthor.com.

## About the Illustrator

Jeffrey Dale turned a part-time job at a small print shop into full-time employment in artistic design, when a career in professional soccer wasn't in the cards. Jeff took his first step toward artistic design after his boss, knowing that he had a background in art, asked him to design a logo for a client. That introduction led to the discovery of his true passion and motivated an education in the design world of Washington, DC. His wide scope of interest and talent inspires him to design and build just about anything one can conceive of creating, including this, his debut children's book.

Jeff is the founder of Dale Design, situated within the thriving design community of Raleigh, North Carolina, where he lives with his wife and two grown children. Learn more about Jeff's creations at www.daledesign.com.

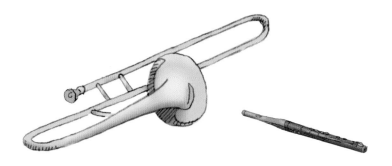

*To my precious grandchildren,*

*Jayden and Olivia.*

*Remember to hold hands*

*and be each other's best friend.*

*Your love and support of one another*

*will color the rainbows.*

*CR*

*To all children,*

*may the sound of your heartbeat*

*color the rainbow for all to enjoy.*

*JD*

I wonder if you can imagine
just how lovely it would be
to create a color in the rainbow
for all the world to see?

"How silly!" you'd say.
"Just how could that be,
to create something so special
by just being me?"

Well, allow me to tell you
a story I recall:
a tale of boldness and joy
and a love shared by all.

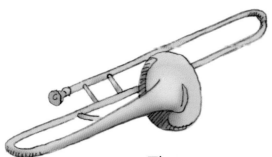

There once was a child
who made music alone;
quite content was he playing,
his big brass trombone.

The sounds he created
were deep, rich, and strong.
How he loved the horn's voice—
such low notes in the songs!

But the boy often wondered:

Was there more to be heard?

Other voices perhaps?

Would that be so absurd?

Then, one day, through his window
came a sound high and sweet,
dancing over his low notes,
on light, sprightly feet.

This beautiful voice,
a new instrument's sound,
moved the boy to declare:
"Every voice must be found!"

Playing his horn through the streets

so that others might hear,

he played loud and strong,

to draw others near.

The first voice to answer
the trombone's deep call
was the sweet little piccolo,
ready to give it her all!

Together, they played:

"Lend your voice! Play your part!

Something grand is beginning—

join us for the start!"

Neighbors' doors opened wide
with kids eager to play.
They showed off their instruments
in a colorful display.

The bagpipe from Scotland
was high pitched and humming,
and the janguu from Korea
had two tones of drumming.

The trumpet when blown
gave cheeks a pink glow.
Guitars strummed so gently;
French horns murmured low.

The strings sang a melody
with the flutes high and sweet,
and oboes crooned softly,
gentle lullabies for sleep.

Each instrument's voice
made a sound like no other.
Creating music together
was a joy to discover!

The music rang out
as they all harmonized.
But something was changing,
and to their surprise,

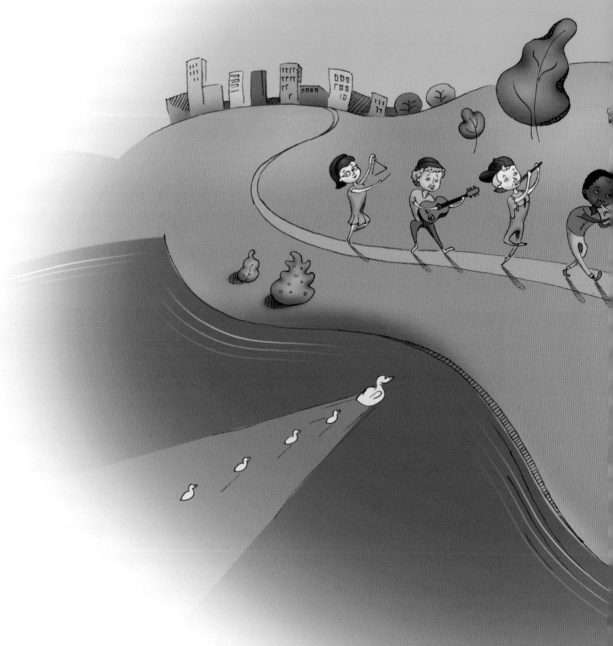

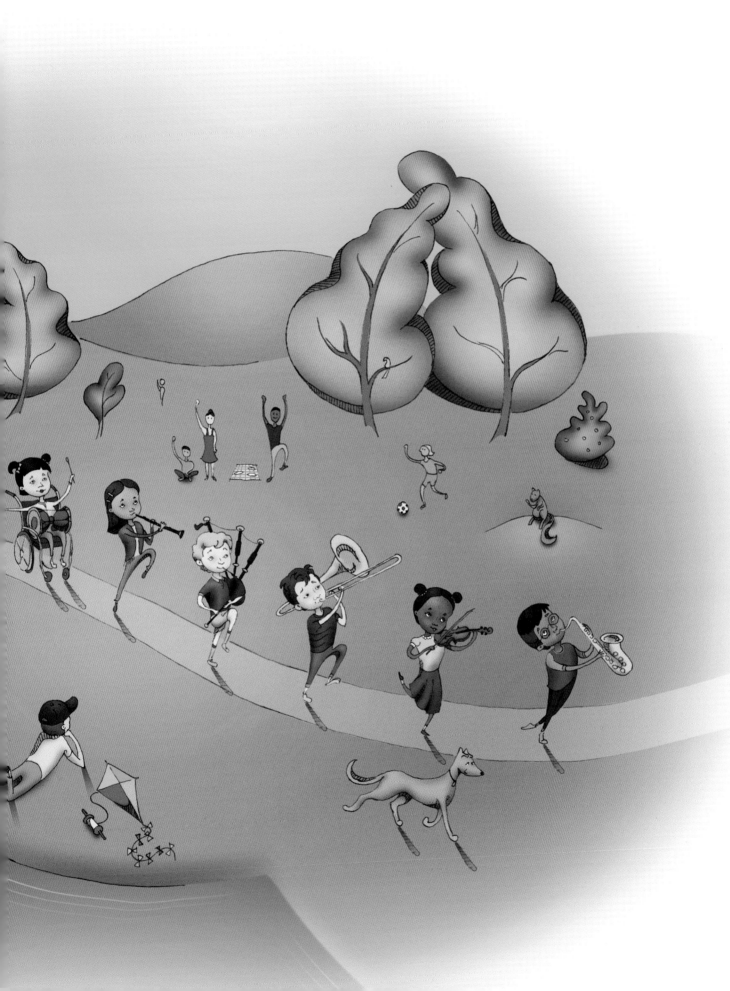

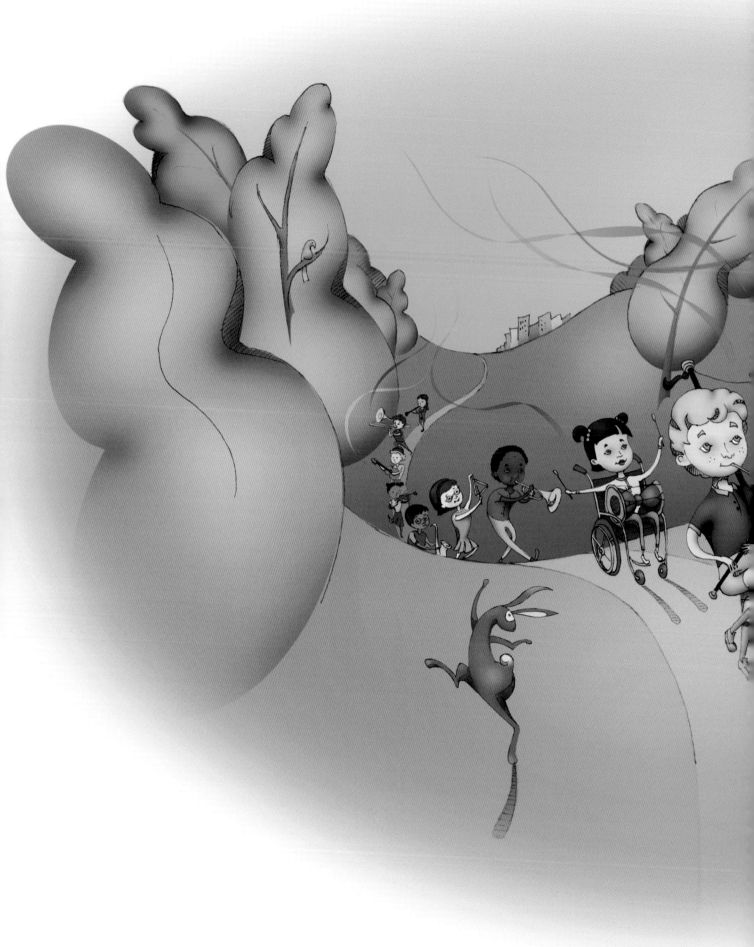

a miracle came forth
from each instrument played,
shooting colors aloft
in a joyous display!

As the children's bright music
danced on the breeze,
their notes swirled like ribbons
flying graceful and free.

The ribbons lifted skyward,
rising higher and higher,
forming bands of bright colors
for all to admire.

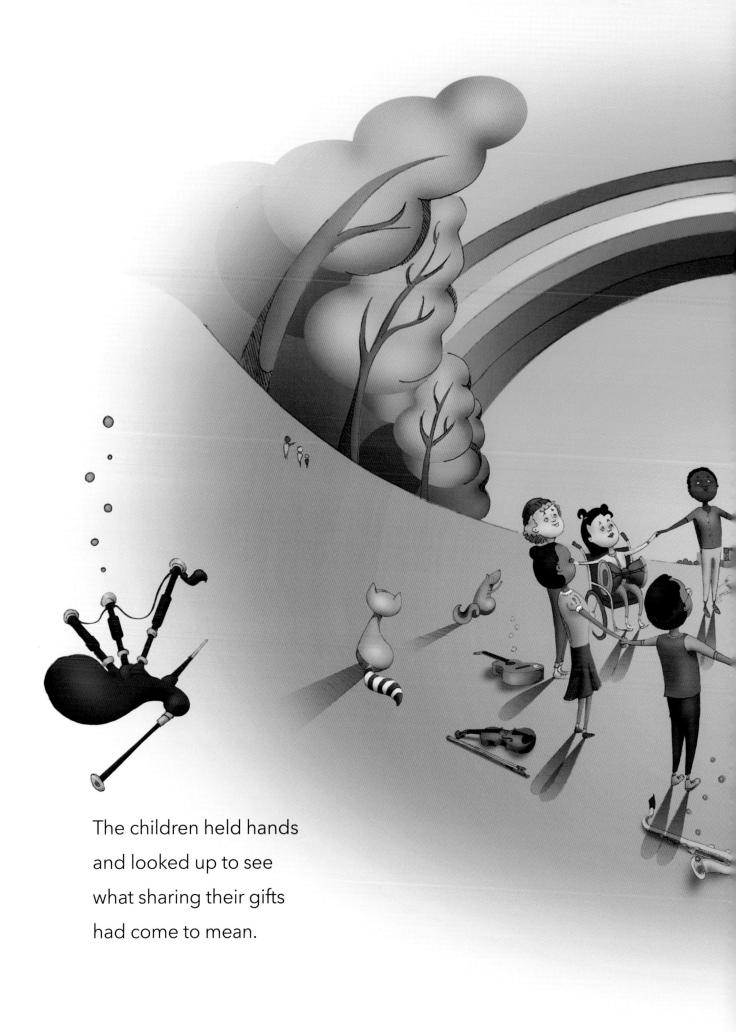

The children held hands
and looked up to see
what sharing their gifts
had come to mean.

With each single instrument
playing its part,
a rainbow had formed
from the song of each heart.

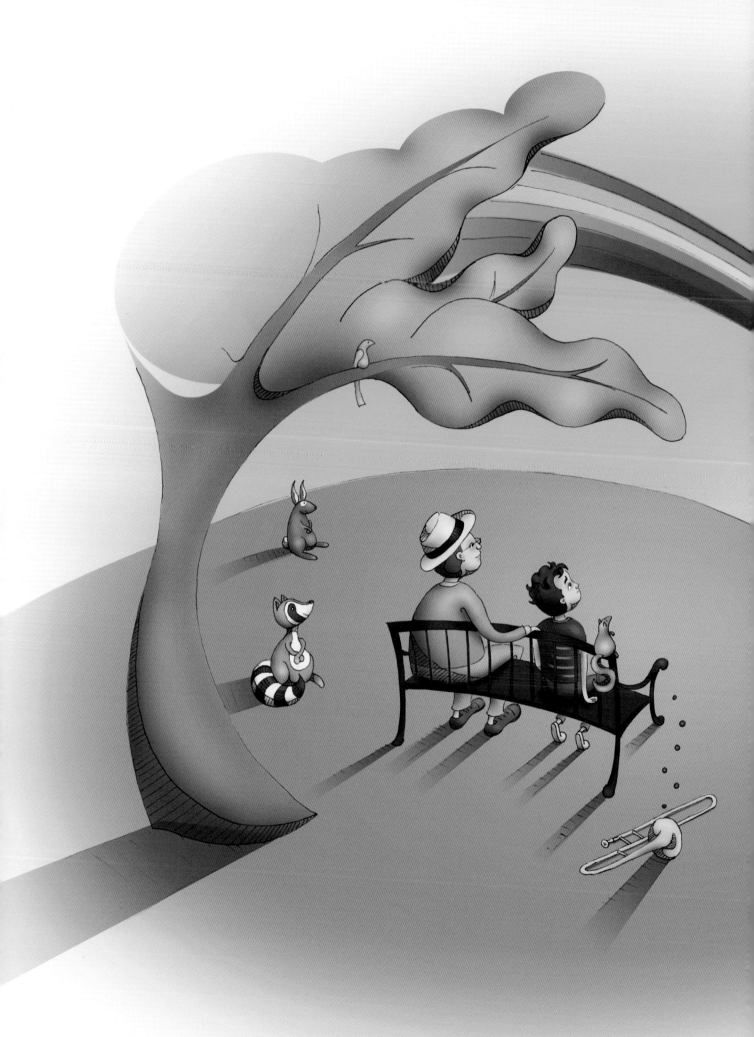

Children sharing and celebrating
what makes each one unique:
creating harmony from differences—
that's the miracle we seek.

Coloring the Rainbow © 2023 by Welcome Ohm LLC. All rights reserved. No part of this book may be reproduced in any form whatsoever, by photography or xerography or by any other means, by broadcast or transmission, by translation into any kind of language, nor by recording electronically or otherwise, without permission in writing from the author, except by a reviewer, who may quote brief passages in critical articles or reviews.

Beaver's Pond Press is committed to turning interesting people into independent authors. In that spirit, we are proud to offer this book to our readers; however, the story, the experiences, and the words are the author's alone.

Written by Catherine Rose
Illustrated by Jeffrey Dale
Book design and typesetting by Dale Design

ISBN 13: 978-1-64343-637-1
Library of Congress Catalog Number: 2023904246
Printed in the United States of America
First Edition: 2023
27 26 25 24 23        5 4 3 2 1

Beaver's Pond Press
939 Seventh Street West
Saint Paul, MN 55102
(952) 829-8818
www.BeaversPondPress.com

To order, visit www.catherinerose-childauthor.com. Reseller discounts available.

Contact Catherine Rose at www.catherinerose-childauthor.com for school and library visits, speaking engagements, book club discussions, blog content, and interviews.

Contact Jeffrey Dale at www.daledesign.com for interviews.